Enid Blyton's

The Little Bear's Adventure

ILLUSTRATED BY MARIO CAPALDI

A TEMPLAR BOOK

Produced by The Templar Company plc, Pippbrook Mill, London Road, Dorking, Surrey RH4 1JE, Great Britain.

Text copyright © *The Bear and the Duck* 1926-1953 by Darrell Waters Limited
This edition illustration and design copyright © 1996 by The Templar Company plc
Enid Blyton's signature mark is a registered trademark of Darrell Waters Limited

This edition produced for Parragon Books, Units 13-17, Avonbridge Trading Estate, Atlantic Road, Avonmouth, Bristol BS11 9QD

This book contains material first published as *The Bear and the Duck* in Enid Blyton's Sunny Stories
and Sunny Stories between 1926 and 1953.

Printed and bound in Italy

ISBN 0-75251-461-X

‖ •PARRAGON• ‖

Once upon a time there was a little brown bear. He lived on the top shelf in the toyshop, with his best friend, a duck. They had been there for a whole year. Fancy that! A whole year!

They were very unhappy about it. They got dustier and dustier, and had almost given up hope of ever being sold. They longed to have a little boy or girl to own them.

You see, by some mistake, the duck had a bear's growl and the bear had a duck's quack. It was most upsetting. Whenever the bear was squeezed in his middle, he said "Quack!" very loudly indeed – and whenever the duck was squeezed she said "Grr-rrrr!"

The shopkeeper had tried to sell them, but she couldn't, and so she had put them away on the top shelf.

One day a little girl came
into the shop with her
mother. She had come to
spend the money that
her granny had given
her for her birthday.

"I want a bear and a duck," she said. Then she pointed up to the shelf. "Oh, look!" she said. "There's a lovely little brown bear, and he has a duck right next to him."

The shopkeeper took them down – how excited the bear and duck felt when they thought they might be sold to this nice little girl!

"Do they say anything?" she asked.

"Well," said the shopkeeper, "it's rather funny. The bear quacks like a duck, and the duck growls like a bear. A mistake was made, and it is impossible to put it right."

The little girl pressed the bear

and he made a quack loudly. Then she pressed the duck and it had to growl – "Grr-rrrr!"

"Oh," said the little girl, disappointed, "what a pity! They make the wrong sounds. I'm afraid I don't want them."

The little bear was quite upset. He put a comforting paw on duck's shoulder. The little girl looked at them again, and they looked so sad that she felt quite sorry for them.

"I'd like to get a bear that growls properly and a duck that quacks in the right way," she said. "But if I can't I might come back and buy these two."

"Very well," said the shopkeeper, and she put the two toys back on the top shelf again. They watched the little girl go out of the shop. They felt most unhappy. To think they could have gone to live with a nice girl like that.

That night the bear spoke to the duck. "Quack!" he said. "Duck, listen to me. It's quite time we did something to help ourselves."

"Grr-rrrr!" said the duck. "We will go to the Little Wise Woman on the hill," said the bear, "and ask for her help. Maybe she can do something for us." He jumped down from the shelf, went over to the window which was open at the bottom, and jumped through.

"Come on Duck," he called, and duck waddled out behind him across the wet grass.

After a long walk, they came to the hill where the Little Wise Woman lived. Her cottage was at the top, and the two toys could see that it was brightly lit.

The Little Wise Woman was having a party, but just as the two toys approached, the guests began to leave. Out went Dame Big-Feet, the witch, on her broomstick. Out went Mrs Twinkle, the plump, jolly woman who sold balloons, and Mr Poker-Man, who was as tall and as thin as a poker. Last of all went Roll-Around, who was as round as a ball, and rolled along instead of walking.

The two toys hid outside until all the goodbyes were said, and then they crept out. They peered in at the window, and to their great surprise they saw the Little Wise Woman sitting on a chair, groaning and crying.

"Oh my!" she said. "I'm so tired, and there's all this mess to clear up before I go to bed."

The bear felt sorry for the unhappy little woman. He knocked on the door and went in.

"We will clear up everything for you," he said. "Don't worry. My friend duck will make you a nice cup of tea, and a hot-water bottle, and I will sweep up the mess, clear the table, and wash up."

The Little Wise Woman was so surprised that she didn't know what to say.

"Where have you two come from?" she asked at last. "And why have you come to visit me tonight?" "Never mind," said the bear, deciding not to talk about his own troubles now. "Why don't you snuggle into bed. Leave the rest to us."

"Grr-rrrr!" growled the duck kindly, much to the Little Wise Woman's surprise.

"Quack!" said the bear, and surprised her still more. Then she remembered that her friend, the toyshop woman, had told her about a bear who quacked and a duck who growled, and she thought these must be the two strange toys. How kind they were to come and look after her like this, just when she had so much clearing up to do!

While the Little Wise Woman was getting ready for bed, the duck made a nice cup of tea, and gave her a hot-water bottle.

The bear was very busy, too. He cleared all the dirty dishes, washed them up, put them neatly away, and swept the floor. Then he put the cakes into their tins and the biscuits into their jars, and put the lids on.

He was very hungry, but of course

he didn't dream of taking even half a biscuit. He knew it would be wrong, and he was a very good little bear.

"She's almost asleep," said the duck, peeking around the bedroom door. "We'd better go."

"I'm not quite asleep," said the Little Wise Woman, in a drowsy voice. "Before you go, look in my kitchen drawer. You will find two boxes of magic sweets there. Bear, take a yellow sweet, Duck, take a blue one. You won't be sorry you came to help me tonight."

"Thank you," said the bear, astonished.

He knew that the Little Wise Woman had many marvellous spells, and he wondered what would happen when he and the duck swallowed the magic sweets.

Perhaps he would grow beautiful whiskers, and maybe the duck would grow a wonderful tail.

He took a yellow sweet, and the duck swallowed a blue one. Then they carefully shut the kitchen drawer, called goodnight to the Little Wise Woman and went out into the night.

They were very tired when they
got back to the toyshop. They
climbed up to their shelf, leaned
back against the wall, and fell fast
asleep at once.

They didn't wake up until the sun was shining into the shop. The doorbell woke them with a jump and they sat up. They saw the same little girl who had come to the shop the day before. She looked up at their shelf and pointed to them.

"I've come back to see that bear and duck again." she said.

The shopkeeper lifted them down. "It *is* a pity the duck growls and the bear quacks," she said.

She pressed the duck in the middle – and to everyone's enormous surprise the duck said "Quack!" very loudly indeed. The most surprised of all was the duck herself. She had never in her life said "Quack", and it felt very funny indeed.

Then the little girl squeezed the bear, and to his delight he growled!

"Grr-rrrr!" he went. Just like that.

"What a funny thing," said the

little girl. "Have you had them mended?"

"No," said the shopkeeper, just as surprised as the little girl. "They've not been taken down from their shelf since you went out of the shop. I can't think what has happened to them."

The little girl pressed the bear and the duck again. "Grr-rrrr!" growled the bear. "Quack!" said the duck. They were both most

delighted. So *that* was what the pills from the Little Wise Woman had done – given them the right voices!

"Well, I will buy them now," said the little girl. "There's nothing wrong with them at all, and they are just what I wanted. I think the bear is lovely and the duck is a dear. I shall love them very much."

How pleased the two toys were when they heard that! When the shopkeeper popped them into a

box, they hugged one another hard
– so hard that the duck had to say
"Quack!" and the bear had to say
"Grr-rrrr!"

"Listen to that!" said the little
girl, laughing. "They're saying that
they're glad to come home with me."

The duck and the bear are very happy indeed now, and you should just hear the duck say "Quack!" and the bear say "Grr-rrrr!" whenever the little girl plays with them. They have quite the loudest voices in the playroom.